DATE DUE

			PRINTED IN U.S.A.

Picasso

Text by
ROBERT FISHER

Edited by
THEODORE REFF
Associate Professor of Art History
Columbia University

TUDOR PUBLISHING COMPANY
New York

Published by

TUDOR PUBLISHING COMPANY

New York, 1967

Library of Congress Catalog Card Number: 66-10560

Printed in Japan

PICASSO, THE PERENNIAL

A pioneer in the history of modern art and a controversial proponent of independence, both artistic and political, Pablo Ruiz Picasso represents, more than any other living artist, the changing moods and passions of our times. Now in his eighties, he is as much the center of controversy and comment as ever, though he has been a painter for 75 years. Wherever artists, critics and art enthusiasts gather, there can be no argument that he sits enthroned on Mt. Parnassus, the sacred home of the muses. Exponent of the abstract, inventor of cubism and master of surrealism, he has branched out from painting into sculpture, ceramics and politics, and excelled in all but the last. And this incredible man, who once boasted that he always looked straight into the sun, who has never tried to shield himself from controversy, and who long ago plunged into life with enthusiasm abundant, is still experimenting with new art forms and new ideas.

Born in Malaga, Spain, Picasso was reared in a family devoted to art. From the time of his birth on October 25, 1881, the boy was surrounded by the paintings of his father, José Ruiz Blasco, and nurtured in an appreciation of elegance by his mother, Maria Picasso Lopez, daughter of a prominent Malaga family. Like all Spanish children, he took the names of both his father and mother. (His father was the son of a man named Ruiz and a woman of the Blasco family; thus, Pablo Ruiz y Picasso, later shortened by dropping the "y", "and".)

Family background

By 1889, Picasso was painting under his father's direction, and by 1891, when his family moved to Corunna, on the Atlantic coast of Spain, was already recognized as a possible genius. Before leaving this bleak town for a better post elsewhere, Picasso's father further encouraged him and arranged to have his works shown at a local general store. In 1895, after settling in Barcelona where his father had a new job teaching at the School of Fine Arts, Pablo took the entrance examinations for the school, and although much younger than usual passed with highest marks. He was hailed as a prodigy, and the professors undertook with great eagerness to mold the fifteen-year-old boy into another dull academic painter.

Early training

Two years later, under the patronage of a wealthy uncle, Pablo entered the Royal Academy in Madrid, recommended not only by his promise but by the prizes he had already won in Madrid and Malaga. He led a fairly customary life for a young artist of the time, dissipating himself and getting into trouble with teachers and friends, until he was eventually cut off by his rich uncle. Suffering from illness and near starvation, he struggled to remain in Madrid, but in 1900 was finally forced to give up the attempt and return, still only nineteen years old, to his parents in Barcelona.

Paris, Malaga, Madrid

In the autumn of 1900, eager to sample the life of Paris, Picasso traveled to France with a companion, Carlos Casagemas, with whom he lived for a while in the City of Light. By Christmas, with Casagemas desperately ill and Picasso running out of money, the two returned to Malaga, where Picasso hoped to restore his friend's health and find a new source of inspiration for his own paintings. Within ten days, however, they had also to leave Malaga, having incurred the wrath of Picasso's relatives, who were disturbed by Picasso's Bohemian airs, his friend's untidiness and the pair's irreverent attitude. They fled to Madrid, where, after dropping Casagemas at a tavern, a familiar and

4

beloved scene of respite for that lover of wine, Picasso set up a studio for himself, and in conjunction with another friend, published a few issues of a new journal, *Young Art*. This collapsed for lack of support, and in May Picasso left for Paris a second time, via Barcelona.

"Young Art"

In the French capital, Picasso began to paint furiously, and found a sponsor, a Catalonian named Mañach. This congenial businessman took Picasso into his apartment, giving him the bigger of two rooms, and bought him paints, canvas and food. By January of 1902, however, after only six months in the city, Picasso became disillusioned, partly because of a general feeling of *malaise* and partly because he was unable to sell any of his works. From January until July, he stayed in Barcelona, existing with the help of his family. In the fall, he decided again that Paris was after all the best place for a young artist, and returned to France. There, a new benefactor, a writer named Max Jacob, shared his room with him, and all seemed well at first. By December, however, still unable to sell any of his paintings, he had again fallen prey to disillusion and, when Jacob lost his job, retreated again to Barcelona. On the eve of his departure, desperate for food and fuel, he burned several of his works in order to keep warm in the cold and lonely garret he and Jacob occupied.

At 21, Picasso began to settle down, and his stay in Barcelona lasted for sixteen months. He painted well during this period, found the money for his own studio, and conducted several love affairs, with his art as well as with the girls of the town. In April, 1904, he returned to Paris for the last time, and took up permanent residence in that city. Shortly after arriving, he met Fernande Oliver, with whom he was to live for eight years, and fell into the company of a small but vocal group of literary and artistic friends. Based in the "Bateau Lavoir (Laundry

Return to Paris —The "Bateau Lavoir"

5

Boat)," a dilapidated building housing a nest of artists and Bohemians in Montmartre, Picasso began to live the life of a true young expatriate in Paris. With his new mistress and friends he was to create an exciting and vigorous way of life which would eventually also find him earning a good income.

The
Steins

Gertrude Stein and her brother, Leo, were among the first of Picasso's devoted patrons. Leo came to his studio one day, and over the protests of Gertrude, purchased *Girl with a Basket of Flowers* (1905). Picasso was to paint Gertrude later in a work which her friends objected to, but which she loved so much she kept it next to her bed until her death after World War II.

Having passed through the melancholy phase known as his Blue Period (1901–04), Picasso now entered his Pink Period (1905–06), a time when he was constantly experimenting with forms and textures in his paintings. But a new and more fruitful period was soon to follow.

"Women of Avignon" and birth of Cubism

A radical departure from all he had previously done, and an epoch-making painting in the history of art, Picasso's *Women of Avignon* (1907) was soundly criticized by all his friends. It was the first painting in which he was entirely himself, although he was evidently influenced by Cézanne and El Greco. Matisse and Apollinaire, particularly, condemmed the work, accusing Picasso of deliberately playing a bad joke on his audience. Some critics felt he was merely passing through a phase of extreme interest in the art of primitive Africa. Only two or three understood that Picasso had just given birth to a new form of art—cubism, the concept of which allegedly originated in the famous passage in Cézanne's letter, published in 1907, in which that master painter had written, "You must see in nature the cylinder, the sphere, and the cone."

For the next few years, becoming more and more famous

and reaping good profits from his work, Picasso continued to paint in a cubist manner, dedicating his talents to this cause almost exclusively until 1917. He spent his summers at various southern resorts, took a new mistress (Eva Gouel), and experimented with collage. During the war, Eva died and toward the end of the holocaust, Picasso turned to other forms of expression, including the designing of costumes and scenery for Diaghilev's Russian Ballet. An enraged audience tried to attack composer, choreographer, artist and performers when the first work, *Parade,* was presented in Paris in May, 1917. The artist, naturally, was delighted with this reaction and promised more of his outrageous efforts to annoy the bourgeoisie.

Ballet designs— "Parade"

In 1918, surprising everyone, he married the ballerina Olga Koklova, but found his happiness dampened when his good friend, the poet Apollinaire, died of influenza on the day the First World War ended. For two or three years after the war, Picasso continued designing ballet costumes and scenery, but in 1923 returned to painting with increasing vigor. A few years earlier, he had begun to experiment with a quasi-Greco-Roman style, resulting in what is now known as his Classical Period. Simultaneously, however, he had continued to paint in a cubistic manner, and had originated his own unique form of synthetic cubism.

Classical Period

By 1925, Picasso had begun to leave cubism behind and was becoming interested in surrealism, whose manifesto had been published the year before by André Breton. When he painted *Three Dancers* in 1925, he was obsessed with the new form. Its tendency toward monstrous distortion appealed to his sense of the bizarre and unnatural in the "real" world around him, and to the mysticism in his Spanish soul. In 1928, still painting in a surrealistic style, he took up sculpture again and the first results, quite nautrally, were also deformed shapes. In 1930–31, he nearly

"Three Dancers" and Surrealism

7

abandoned painting, devoting most of his energy to sculpture.

In the mid-thirties, he also turned to poetry. This was quite natural partly because he had always been a literary painter, tending toward lyrical inspiration and classical themes and references, and partly because most of his earlier days, from the time of his arrival in Paris in 1904, had been spent in the company of poets and authors.

The Paris Circle

Among his early poet friends were not only Apollinaire and Max Jacob, but Alfred Jarry, Pierre Reverdy, Maurice Raynal and Georges Duhamel. Picasso also devoted much time to his friendship with cricus performers and bullfighters, including the great master of the *corrida*, Manolo. Among his other close friends were Ambroise Vollard and Gertrude Stein. As for painters, he was on intimate terms with Matisse, Braque, Derain, Juan Gris, and Fernand Leger.

Eluard and Communism

At about this same time, however, Picasso became somewhat disenchanted with the trivialities of the social life he was leading among the wealthy and celebrity-conscious, and began to withdraw. He renewed an old friendship with the poet Jaime Sabartes, and began to rely more and more on the ideas of the French Communist poet, Paul Eluard. By the time the Civil War in Spain broke out, he was no longer disengaged from world events. Eluard, in a speech in Spain in 1936, had hailed Picasso in these words, "I speak of that which helps me to live, of that which is good," and then, "Picasso wants the truth, the real truth." When Nazi planes bombed the Spanish town of Guernica during the Civil War, Picasso felt impelled to speak the truth.

The Spanish Civil War— Guernica

Shortly before the incident, the artist had been commissioned by the Spanish government to paint a mural for an official exhibit at the world's fair to be held in Paris in the summer of 1937. When news of the bombing, on April 29, reached him, he began to work in a frenzy, completing the gigantic mural in two months. This stirring work, not at all a call to arms against the Fascists, but a condemnation of war as such, instantly made Picasso's name familiar in the few corners of the world where it was as yet unknown. The mural is an attack on all war and all inhumanity, not simply a polemic appeal against Fascism, though the latter was its unwitting father. *"Guernica"*

The immediate prewar period found Picasso at work in Paris, and in the summer, at Mougins or Antibes. His painting, interrupted by a severe attack of sciatica in the winter of 1938–39, was resumed in the summer of the year war broke out; and one day before the Nazis invaded Poland, Picasso finished his great work *Night Fishing at Antibes*. *"Night Fishing at Antibes"*

The war years are puzzling, as Picasso was allowed to live and work peacefully in Paris throughout the Nazi occupation. Most critics feel that the Nazis hesitated to harm him because of his international reputation and immense following, even in Axis and Axis-satellite countries. Whatever the reason, they left him alone, permitting him to spend the period "harmlessly" painting still-life scenes and portraits of Dora Maar, writing the play "Desire Caught by the Tail," and sculpting. He was not allowed to exhibit, of course, and was frequently attacked by such conservatives as Vlaminck, who took advantage of the anti-cubist and anti-surrealist campaign fostered by the German authorities to castigate his achievements. *World War II*

When Paris was liberated, a horde of American and British fans of Picasso, worried about his fate during the final days of the Allied invasion of France, stormed his apartment on the rue des Grands Augustins. The first to reach him on the morning of August 24, 1944, was Lee Miller, a female war correspondent for *Vogue*. Picasso welcomed her with tears of joy in his eyes, delighted to find that the first Allied "soldier" to liberate him turned out to be a woman.

The war ended, Picasso was free to turn again to the south and his beloved Mediterranean of color and sun. With Francoise Gilot, he moved to Antibes and began again to paint, to make lithographs by the scores, and to sculpt. When the French government opened a National Museum of Modern Art, Picasso contributed ten of his works. He also gave many works to the Grimaldi Museum in Antibes, which was rechristened the Picasso Museum in his honor. He began to exhibit more frequently, in French provincial towns as well as elsewhere throughout the free world.

Sculpture and lithography

Having joined the Communist Party in late 1944, mostly under the influence of his friend, Paul Eluard, Picasso was called upon by Communist peace groups and other front organizations to contribute to their campaigns against American and Western policies in the post-war period. As a result, he not only provided these movement with a new emblem—the dove of peace—but made long journeys to their propaganda conferences to lend his name and prestige to their efforts.

Political involvement

He attended the first three meetings of the World Peace Congress, held in Warsaw, Paris and Sheffield, England, in 1948, 1949 and 1950, respectively. Hating to travel, he nevertheless went to them all, even braving severe British criticism to attend the last of these meetings, which was held after the outbreak of the Korean War and the commitment of British troops in support of the United Nations forces. However, at Sheffield, characteristically, he spoke not of politics, but of his ideas about painting, and he spoke only for a minute. Today it seems clear that Picasso's involvement with the Communists was less that of the revolutionary or ideologue than that of a man grateful to his

The World Peace Congresses

10

friends who happened to be Communists and thankful to the French Communist Party for its stand against the Nazis.

In 1947 and 1949, Francoise Gilot gave birth to two children, a son, Claude, and a daughter, Paloma. Picasso became more and more immersed in family life and almost completely absorbed in peaceful compositions, landscapes, portraits and his continuing work with ceramics and sculpture. In the summer of 1952, he spent two marathon-like months painting murals of *War* and *Peace* for the chapel at Vallauris, where he now maintained a villa. The beasts of War are balanced by a Pegasus of Peace. The chapel is now called the Temple of Peace by the local inhabitants, and the work has an overwhelming effect on visitors. *Family life-ceramics*

Picasso's happiness was not to be perpetual, unfortunately. In November, 1953, his good friend Paul Eluard died and earlier that year Francoise had left him, taking the children with her. After brooding for some time, he met Jacqueline Roque, who helped him to forget the past and to turn toward his new passion, ceramics, with even greater gusto. In 1955, overwhelmed by his role as a famous man, Picasso finally had to take up permanent residence outside Paris, forsaking his old custom of wintering there and spending summers at his villa on the Mediterranean. Moving to La Californie, an Edwardian villa outside Cannes, he relied on Jacqueline to make the place liveable, but in 1958, he moved again, this time purchasing a huge property some fifty miles away. Picasso found to his surprise that because the Chateau de Vauvenargues was the property's center, he had purchased a name as well, and was now entitled to be known as the Marquis de Vauvenargues. Needless to say, he has ignored the whole matter and is doubtless known by this appellation only to the loyal tenants on his land. *The Mediter-ranean*

For a while, he commuted between the new chateau and

11

*Marriage
to Jacque-
line
Roque* La Californie, but a few years after, he abandoned the
Cannes villa and took a new one, Le Mas Notre Dame de
Vie, near Mougins. In March, 1961, still surprising everyone, he married Jacqueline Roque.

Public interest in Picasso's life was revived when his
former mistress, the artist Francoise Gilot, published her
book, *Life with Picasso,* telling for the first time what it
was like to live with this man of genius. Picasso countered
with a lawsuit, and all France was amused by the controversy, somewhat pleased with a man in his eighties who
could yet provoke a *scandale d'amour.*

Still active and productive, Picasso defies definitive
analysis. How can we judge him, or presume to comment
on his meaning, when he is still leading a vigorous life,
*The man
and his
times* changing his concepts of art and his manner of expression?
A perfect champion of twentieth-century manners and mor-
als Picasso has faithfully reflected, in his own way, the tri-
als and glories of our age. Since this is a rapidly-changing
period in which we live, it is natural that the artist should
be as inconstant in his devotion to forms and themes as
Picasso has been. The master of cubism, the champion of
surrealism, is now devoting his time to other principles and
interpretations. Where it will all lead cannot be guessed.
That his present work will prove to be inspiring and com-
pelling is taken for granted, knowing the man, knowing the
times and knowing the way in which he has always risen
to meet opportunity and challenge face to face. Picasso,
who claims that he always looks directly into the sun, also
looks directly at the world and paints the truth as he sees it.

ROBERT FISHER

NOTES ON THE COLOR PLATES

1. *Gypsy Girl on the Beach.* 1898. Oil. Paris, Private Collection. Picasso's unusual sense of composition and his balanced use of colors is already evident in this work, painted when he was only seventeen.

2. *The Embrace.* 1900. Oil. Moscow, Pushkin State Museum of Fine Arts. Painted in the same year that Picasso made his first trip to Paris, this work shows hints of the influence of Lautrec and the Impressionists. Picasso's first sojourn in the City of Light was to last only three months.

3. *Bibi la Purée.* 1901. Oil and wood. Paris, Private Collection The rough brush of the Impressionists is observed here, as is the manner in which color is applied. This pathetic actor and Bohemian has no future career, Picasso is clearly saying. His vanity and pride are to no avail—he is still pitiful.

4. *The Bullfight.* 1901. Oil. Paris, Private Collection. Applying his paints in broad areas of bright and luminous color, Picasso depicts a bullfight in the spring. By June of this year, he has decided to return to Paris to live, his native Spain no longer holding any attraction for him.

5. *Child Holding a Dove.* 1901. Oil. London, Private Collection. His gift as a graphic artist is shown here in this fine example of the paintings of his Blue Period (1901–04). Outlining the child with strong and deep lines, Picasso made the line, an unnatural element, an integral part of his work. His love for children and maternal love will remain with him for decades.

6. *Figure of Jaime Sabartes.* 1901. Moscow, Museum of Western Art. The sad and negative aspect of the model's appearance, the depressing blues, are characteristic of the Blue Period at its first peak of maturity. Sabartes was a close friend of Picasso's and an aspiring poet. Picasso had spied Sabartes waiting alone in a cafe and had rushed home

to paint this picture of the nervous young Spaniard, nearsightedly staring about, hoping to see a friendly face.

7. *The Blue Room.* 1901. Oil. Washington, Phillips Gallery. This is Picasso's own room on the boulevard de Clichy. Given to him by his Spanish benefactor, Manach, it circumscribed the artist's life for the six or seven months he remained in Paris during his second sojourn there. The influence of Toulouse-Lautrec, often referred to, is only a reference to the fact that a copy of a Lautrec poster painted by Picasso hangs over the bed (the middle picture). The poster shows the dancer May Milton in her best form.

8. *Still Life on a Table.* 1901. Oil. Barcelona, Musem of Modern Art. Typical of his early enthusiasm in Paris are such works as this, filled with busy, bright colors and becoming more and more complicated. A critic noted of this work when it was displayed in June, in Paris, "Like all true painters, he adores color for its own sake....he is in love with every object....the flowers that burst forth vigorously toward the light, the vase itself, and the table on which the vase rests."

9. *Woman's Face.* 1901. Oil. Otterlo, Rijksmuseum Kröller-Müller. This urbane portrait of a city woman shows the influence of Renoir in its coloring, but in its somewhat decadent air speaks more of Toulouse-Lautrec. Hints of the dots and dashes of the Pointillists are evident here, but we do not see the luminous air about which Picasso's friends raved so ecstatically during this period.

10. *Mother and Child.* 1902–03. Pastel. Private Collection. Emotions of sadness and depression crowd out a mere hint of simple charm in this brooding work. His style was definitely changing and a growing depression, indeed, would soon force him to leave Paris for the second time and return to Spain.

11. *Mother and Child.* 1903. Pastel. Barcelona, Museum of Modern Art. Made more poignant than ever by the cheerless blue monochromed background is this portrait of a poor mother, a recurring theme of Picasso's Blue Period. Having returned to Paris a third time and having fled again when poverty and depression sent him back to his beloved

sunny southland, Picasso was in no mood for cheerful, light painting.

12. *Celestina*. 1903. Oil. Private Collection. Throughout his life, Picasso was to be acutely interested in the plight of the blind. During his stay in Spain in 1903–04, he sought out the afflicted and painted several portraits in this vein. Picasso once went so far as to suggest that the eyes of painters should be put out, as is done to goldfinches to make them sing more sweetly. The results, he said, would be better paintings.

13. *Acrobat on a Ball*. 1904–05. Oil. Moscow, Pushkin State Museum of Fine Arts. From the Blue Period's inactivity and sadness, Picasso moved slowly toward brighter colors and more active emotions. The juxtaposition of the lithe young girl and the thickly-set athlete makes an excellent composition.

14. *Girl with a Basket of Flowers*. 1905. Oil. Gertrude Stein Collection. Painted during his transition from the Blue to the Pink Period, this shows Picasso's new devotion to color and the triumph of his emotions over academic platitudes. Purchased by Leo Stein over his sister's objections the year it was painted, this was the first of many Picasso's acquired by the Steins. Picasso was grateful to these early patrons, who helped him achieve financial stability during the early days of his fourth sojourn in Paris, to which he had returned in 1904.

15. *Seated Harlequin*. 1905. Oil. Paris, Private Collection. Despite changes in color, his technique remained quite similar to that of the Blue Period. Picasso was to remain infatuated with the idea of himself as a harlequin for years, and the figure of the clown pops up again and again through all his periods.

16. *Two Nudes*. 1906. Oil. Switzerland, Private Collection. Painted perhaps as a result of his trip to Holland, where he was amazed at the size of the voluptuous Dutch girls. This is one of several works on the same theme painted in late 1905 and early 1906.

17. *Peach-colored Nude*. 1906. Oil. Painted just before the *Women of Avignon* (Plate 18) and after he had become interested in nudes and semi-classical studies again, this shows Picasso in an experimental mood.

15

18. *Women of Avignon.* 1907. Oil. New York, Museum of Modern Art. An epoch-making painting, often called the first cubist work. In this radical piece, Picasso is entirely himself, despite the apparent influence of Cézanne, El Greco and Negro sculpture. Criticized by his friends as "outrageous," the work shocked the art world. Some collectors declared that Picasso was now lost to the world of French art. Matisse and Apollinaire condemned the work, the former denouncing Picasso as a fraud who was deliberately playing a bad joke on the modernist movement. In this painting, the woman at left, shown drawing back a curtain to expose her sisters to view, seems quite Egyptian in nature, while the two ladies in the center appear rather Spanish. Those at right, of course, are the blending, the mixture of the two, the first cubist portrayals. The name was given the picture only many years after it was painted, and in allusion to the Calle Avignon in the red-light district of Barcelona.

19. *Flowers on a Table.* 1907. Oil. New York, Private Collection. From this year on, Picasso was to be a confirmed cubist, but after 1917, he began to lose interest in that school of painting. Traces of cubism remain in his works to the present, however. The same primitive African works which influenced Picasso's faces of the two women on the right in the *Women of Avignon* are here very much in evidence. The wood-carvings and masks of French Africa helped him to realize the kind of fantasy he longed to portray on his canvases. He was also beginning to think of sculpting in this period, and this composition is solid enough to be a statue.

20. *Head of a Girl.* 1907. Oil. Paris, Private Collection. Another face painted under the influence of African woodcarvings. Only hints of cubism are evident here, but already the denial of old attitudes of the Impressionists is stressed. Picasso's interest in Iberian masks is also thought to have had some influence on this painting.

21. *Still Life with Gourd.* 1909. Oil. Paris, Private Collection. More and more, Picasso ignores perspective, thinking only of the individual shapes, their lines and their integration with one another. A kind of

Green Period began in 1908, lasting until 1909, during which he seemed fascinated with green colors and their luminosity.

22. *Pensive Harlequin.* 1909. Oil. Paris, Private Collection. Quite similar to his portrait of Georges Braque, also done in 1909, this fine example of analytical cubism shows clearly what kind of development will come next. In this painting, as in that of Braque, Picasso cared very little about what the subject actually looked like....he simply wanted to portray faces in a cubistic manner.

23. *Girl with Mandolin.* 1910. Oil. New York, Private Collection. The lack of color here does not detract from this work's forcefulness, as we can see how much energy Picasso has poured into his cubistic analysis as a means of painting a portrait. The artist left the painting unfinished when his model, exasperated with prolonged sitting, refused to pose in any further sessions. No clearer illustration of the transformation of a straight portrait into cubistic terms can be found than this profound work.

24. *Seated Woman in Armchair.* 1913. Oil. Zurich, J. Eichman Collection. The development of cubism took many forms, including this kind of abstraction in which flat surfaces shown at different angles look rather like collage works. *Papier collé* works were also the subject of some experiments during this prewar period. Also known as *Woman in a Chemise,* this is a highly erotic work which presages many of the paintings Picasso is to do in the 1930's.

25. *Violin.* 1913. Oil. Bern, Hermann Rupf Foundation. Now, the metamorphosis of "real" objects into cubistic abstrations takes on a different form—larger, flat planes of colors are interspersed with each other in a three-dimensional manner. Cubism here takes on an entirely new air. When Apollinaire published several cubist pictures by Picasso in a journal of which he had just become editor, nearly all its subscribers, enraged at what they regarded the bad taste or worse sense of humor of the editor, cancelled their subscriptions.

26. *The Card Player.* 1913–14. Oil. New York, Museum of Modern Art. Similar to *Violin* (Plate 25) in its construction, but more com-

plicated, this shows more of Picasso's personality than the former painting. During the few years preceding the First World War, Picasso became annoyed with his fans and critics who wanted to know the meaning of every new work and the influences which they imagined hidden behind his paintings, and he tended to withdraw somewhat from his usual gregarious existence.

27. *Ma Jolie*. 1914. Oil. Paris, Private Collection. One of several paintings on the same theme, showing a tendency away from strict cubist principles, and somehow less deliberate than *Violin* or *The Card Player* (Plates 25 and 26, respectively). The painting was designed to show his love for a new mistress, Eva Gouel; the words "Ma Jolie" are from a song very popular in Paris in 1914.

28. *Still Life before Open Window*. 1915. Oil. Paris, Private Collection. Brooding forest, planes and angles in a jumbled composition remind the viewer of the collage works of the period. During the first years of the war, Picasso tended to paint with more strict adherence to form, using as his favorite subjects, guitars, a woman in a chair, or still-life groups such as this.

29. *Italian Woman*. 1917. Oil. Switzerland, Private Collection Italian themes, ranging from St. Peter's to 18th-century ballet and even depicting the map of the country, show a tendency to return to realism. During this same year, in Italy, Picasso designs costumes and scenery for the Russian Ballet, produced by the great Diaghilev.

30. *Seated Harlequin*. 1918. Oil. New York, Museum of Modern Art. Picasso's tendency toward what he regarded as classicism was speeded up somewhat by his trip to Italy. Rather than classicism, however, the term "realism" might be more appropriate in this case.

31. *The Balcony*. 1919. Oil. New York, Museum of Modern Art. Picasso's second thoughts about the universality of cubism are hinted at in this blending of his own form of cubism with certain elements of the rococo. During the immediate post-war years, Picasso was immersed in the work of designing three ballets for Diaghilev, and also devoted a great amount of his energies to painting portraits of many friends and

acquaintances in the world of arts and literature. Quite similar to *Table in Front of Window,* painted the same year (Private Collection, Lucerne).

32. *School Girl.* 1919. Oil. London, Douglas Cooper Collection. Pure cubism on many planes, and one of his most colorful during this period, this portrait is a composite of all his previous essays in this particular genre. Since he was soon to develop more intensively his neo-classical manner, the importance of this work cannot be overestimated.

33. *Still Life on Bureau.* 1919. Oil. Picasso's Private Collection. Perhaps the last still-life work belonging to his period of classical realism, this seems to represent Picasso, the vigorous man tired of inventing, pausing to refresh himself in the quiet order of the neo-academic style.

34. *Two Female Nudes.* 1920. Pastel. London, Douglas Cooper Collection. Done by a Picasso interested in Greco-Roman art, this is one of many such painting that will exist side by side with his cubist-inspired works over a period of several years. Elephantine monuments to maternity and fertility, these women are a throwback to Picasso's interest in the enormously-proportioned Dutch girls he saw in 1905, but more than this, they are indicative of his own fascination with the eternal subject of sex and creativity as expressed through the female form.

35. *Three Women at the Fountain.* 1920. Oil. New York, Museum of Modern Art. Daring the impossible, Picasso treats classical themes with a completely unique mixing of traditional and experimental, creating his own unforgettable style.

36. *Still Life with Bird.* 1920. Pastel. Paris, Private Collection. Produced during his classicist period, this cubistic enterprise shows Picasso's completely individualistic approach to this kind of prosaic subject.

37. *Three Musicians.* 1921. Oil. Philadelphia, Museum of Art. One of Picasso's greatest works, this is a masterpiece of synthetic cubism, yet it was produced during the period which we call his classicist phase. Giving the musicians tiny hands, he tries to emphasize the monumental scale of the painting, which measures over 40 square feet. A similar painting, done in the same year, hangs in New York's Museum of Modern

Art, and many critics believe it to be more refined than the work re-produced here. This was Picasso's first attempt to show three figures in a cubist manner, and is a magnificent achievement in its amazing complexity.

38. *Mother and Child.* 1922. Oil. Baltimore, Museum of Art. One of many in the series on maternity which Picasso drew in 1921 and 1922, this is as realistic as *Three Musicians* was not. One example of the artist's many styles, which he will pursue simultaneously for the next forty years.

39. *Mother and Child.* 1922. Oil. New York, Private Collection. The heaviness of this portrait contrasts completely with Picasso's delicate approach to the same subject in Plate 38. This work is statuesque in manner—the simplicity and grace of his earlier series on the same subject (Plates 10 and 11) has vanished. Inspiration for the renewed interest in motherhood came, as might be expected, by the birth of a son, Paulo, in February, 1921.

40. *Still Life with Fish.* 1922–23. Oil. Paris, National Museum of Modern Art. In the summer of 1922, on the coast of Brittany, Picasso tried to portray a new kind of light on his canvases. These fish, placed on a newspaper, are shown in the light of stripes and patterns, themselves acting as sources of light. Many paintings had to be interrupted (perhaps including this one) when his wife, Olga, became ill and Picasso had to rush her back to Paris for an operation.

41. *Nude.* 1923. Pastel and crayon. Picasso's Private Collection. The works which the artist keeps for himself seem to be those which reflect the academic style or the portraits of his intimates.

42. *Paul Drawing Pictures.* 1923. Oil. Picasso's Private Collection. Paul, familiarly known to the artist and his family as Paulo, was the subject of many works by his famous father. Tenderly done, this portrait shows definite traces of the cubistic technique, especially in the legs, clothes and face of the child.

43. *Paul as Pierrot.* 1925. Oil. Picasso's Private Collection. Four-year-old Paul is seen here in the favorite harlequin costume of his

father. In the same year, Picasso painted his son as a toreador and again as a harlequin, but holding a bunch of flowers.

44. *Still Life with Cake*. 1924. Oil. New York, Museum of Modern Art. The years between 1922 and 1930 were active and peaceful, Picasso centering his life around his wife and their new son. He continued to paint in many styles simultaneously, as in this remarkable work in which his line technique is so beautifully demonstrated.

45. *View of a Port*. 1924. Oil. Belgium, Private Collection. The attempt to harmonize real shapes with cubistic demands may be indicated here. This was probably painted in the summer, which he spent at Juan-les-Pines, in the glare of his beloved southern sun. During this year, he also designed another ballet set, for *Mercure*.

46. *Three Dancers*. 1925. Oil. Picasso's Private Collection. Still able to utilize cubist techniques whenever he wishes, Picasso begins to paint in a surrealistic fashion during this period. He will continue to do so until 1937. After spending some time with Diaghilev and Massine in Monte Carlo in early 1925, he painted this work, which seems to hint at the obscene and deformed monsters which will later come to dominate some of his surrealistic works.

47. *Paul's Face*. 1925. Crayon and pastel. Picasso's Private Collection. The elegance of Picasso's neo-classical draughtsmanship is beautifully represented in this portrait of his son.

48. *Seated Woman*. 1927. Oil. Farmington, Private Collection. One of the first works of many in the same style, this shows a new Picasso, trying out yet another individual style, which will amaze the world of art. The human form is completely transformed into something deeply disquieting, even sinister.

49. *Paul as Pierrot*. 1929. Oil. Picasso's Private Collection. The boy's character seems to be expressed more accurately in this portrait as opposed to the earlier one (Plate 43). Much more realistic, and painted in an obvious attempt to harmonize the colors of subject and background, this is a remarkably tender piece of art.

50. *On the Beach.* 1928. Oil. New York, Museum of Modern Art. Also known as *On the Beach (Dinard)*, from the site where Picasso painted it, this amusing little piece is sympathetic to expressionism, but not completely of it. From 1928, Picasso allowed his humor and whimsey to take him where they would, overwhelmed, perhaps, by his recognition of the danger lurking in his attitude towards surrealism as a mode of self-expression.

51. *The Dream.* 1932. Oil. New York, Private Collection. One of an extraordinary series of portraits of a woman made in this year, this makes an obvious effort to avoid grotesque distortion in the subject's face, even while twisting her body completely out of shape. Picasso's new model was Marie-Thérèse Walter, a girl who lived with him at Boisgeloup, his new studio not far from Paris.

52. *Girl Before a Mirror.* 1932. Oil. New York, Museum of Modern Art. One of the most famous of all Picasso's works, this elaborate composition, in addition to being a masterpiece of surrealism, has a profoundly human insight. The deformation of the real world becomes complete. The model once again is Marie-Thérèse Walter.

53. *Sleeping Nude.* 1932. Oil. Again using Marie-Thérèse as a model, Picasso painted several works like this. In the background, a philodendron springs up, seeming to lean toward the ripe breasts of the sleeping nude. Her arms, her legs, the position of her head, all lead to the central point of attention, the voluptuous breasts and the swan-like neck of the girl.

54. *The Muse.* 1935. Oil. Paris, National Museum of Modern Art. A satirical comment on the artist and his life, this painting shows the return of a certain warmth within the artist. The girl asleep in the background reminds us that this is part of a series of several paintings with the theme of girls asleep or reading, all done during the same period. Faces and legs, in particular, are distorted, ushering in yet another period of extreme distortion which was to reach its climax in *Guernica* (Plate 57).

55. *Face and Pitcher.* 1937. Oil. Perhaps this is one of many

portraits, mostly sketches, which Picasso did of Cecile Eluard, daughter of his old friend, Paul, when they all spent the summer of 1937 at the town of Mougins. It was painted after he had done *Guernica*, and was perhaps a form of relaxation for him after the exhausting work of producing the huge masterpiece (Plate 57).

56. *Portrait of Marie-Thérèse*. 1937. Oil. Private Collection. Begun in 1936, when the subject was still his mistress, but finished in 1937, when she was no longer on the scene, this shows Marie-Thérèse reading. The portrait is one of the most beautiful of all Picasso's surrealistic efforts, but its distortions lead the observer to wonder whether the times were out of joint with the artist.

57. *Guernica*. 1937. Mural. New York, Museum of Modern Art. The apotheosis of surrealism, with Picasso's own cubism to stamp it as unmistakably his, was painted as a protest against the Nazi air force's bombing of Guernica, a small Spanish town, during that nation's civil war. From this time on, Picasso's interest in politics becomes ever more apparent and he will come to regard himself as a considerable source of influence in world public opinion. His art becoming a weapon against the Nazis and Fascists, Picasso was hailed around the world for his courage. The light of truth, held by the woman leaning from the window, shows us the horrible reality of war. The brutal enemy is nowhere in sight. Neither the horse nor the bull symbolize the aggressors, but simply stand for the common brutality of man's inhumanity to man. The simplicity of this painting, together with its timeliness, made it the masterpiece that the world knows it to be.

58. *Portrait of Maia*. 1938. Oil. Picasso's Private Collection. Made more impressive by the use of surrealist distortion, the daughter's face here expresses the great tenderness felt for her by her painter-father.

59. *The Cock.*. 1938. Pastel. New York, Private Collection. The energy and fighting spirit of the cock impressed Picasso, a man of many moods, and he took up the bird as a symbol in many of his works during this period.

60. *Maia's Face*. 1938. Pastel. Picasso's Private Collection. Re-

markably similar to his portrait *Paul's Face* (Plate 47) is this tender expression of love for his daughter.

61. *Girl With a Cock.* 1938. Oil. New York, Private Collection. Some critics feel that this portrait shows Picasso's subconscious alarm at the losing cause of the Spanish loyalists in the civil war. The girl, who is about to kill the bird on her lap, is also considered by some to represent Picasso himself, about to slay a peaceful bird in the throes of a surrealistic fit of of passion.

62. *Cat and Bird.* 1939. Oil. Picasso's Private Collection. Produced just before the outbreak of World War II, the dark and cruel cat, a symbol of war, is devouring the bird, symbol of peace. Picasso had only recently recovered from a severe case of sciatica when he painted this half-human beast of destruction.

63. *Girl Holding a Boat.* 1939. Oil. Picasso's Private Collection. Painted just before *Night Fishing at Antibes* (Plate 64), this work was accomplished at Antibes, the Mediterranean fishing village where Picasso had come to spend the summer of 1939. The surrealistic lessons to be learned from this work are all the more evident because of the child-like manner in which the artist deliberately painted it.

64. *Night Fishing at Antibes.* 1939. Oil. New York, Museum of Modern Art. The mood and composition of this painting, though the subject is a pleasant one, is nevertheless quite similar to that of *Guernica*. The dark colors of fear and anxiety are here overwhelming. Discovering the fishermen luring strange and wonderful sea creatures to the surface by the glare of strong lamps at night, Picasso depicted their spearing of the fish in a major dramatic effort which is pleasing, yet somehow disturbing.

65. *Nude Dressing Her Hair.* 1940. Oil. Picasso's Private Collection. Painted in June, just before Nazi troops occupied Royan, where he was staying, this work betrays Picasso's extreme frustration and anger. The female nude has become a monster ... there is no beauty whatsoever in this work. The artist's despair is complete. Also known as *Seated Woman Dressing Her Hair*.

66. *Skull of Bull on a Table.* 1942. Oil. Paris, Private Collection. Painted in April, this shows the Spanish attitude toward death rather than the brutal air of decomposition which often attracted surrealist painters of other backgrounds. Set against the black night of the Nazi occupation, the grinning skull is particularly frightening because it seems to represent a kind of permanence of death.

67. *Portrait of Dora Maar.* 1943. Oil. Paris, Private Collection. This melody of simple painting portrays Picasso's war-time mistress. During the period 1937–1945, he painted her portrait many times, used her as a model constantly and sketched her figure and profile on hundreds of occasions.

68. *Tomato and Pitcher.* 1944. Oil. Picasso's Private Collection. A scene from the window of Picasso's studio, looking out across the roofs of Paris. The grey facade of Paris and its peaked roofs make a precise cubist background for a semi-surrealistic tomato plant.

69. *Paris Landscape.* 1945. Oil. Picasso's Private Collection. Notre Dame, seen from the banks of the Seine and framed by the arch of a bridge, is the center of this cubistic jumble of buildings and stones. It is a fine example of Picasso's ability to blend cubism with naturalism. With the end of the war, Picasso turned more and more to ceramics and the graphic arts, but perhaps in praise of her liberation, he first painted this scene of the City of Light.

70. *Still Life.* 1945. Oil. Painted in the summer, which Picasso spent in Provence and on the Mediterranean. The drabness of the dark days under the Nazis is replaced by bright and roughly-drawn colors, which show a cheerful determination to leap freely from the canvas.

71. *Joy of Life.* 1946. Mural. Antibes, Grimaldi Museum. Also known as *Wonderful to be Alive* and *Pastoral,* this amazing redrawing of a classical theme represents the artist's hope for a world at peace. The old Greco-Roman rites of spring, represented here by goats, Pan and a dancing Diana, could never have been gayer.

72. *Seated Woman.* 1947. Oil. Picasso's Private Collection. The artist's peaceful life at Antibes, on the Mediterranean coast, is reflected

in this charming work, an abstraction of planes and shapes which form a joyful composition.

73. *Kitchen.* 1948. Oil. Picasso's Private Collection. Though he was preoccupied with new forms of expression, including ceramics, during the period when he painted this, Picasso obviously felt that he could contribute to his attempts to influence the world in peaceful ways by painting domestic scenes. It was in 1948 that he began to be active in promoting Communist peace campaigns.

74. *Claude.* 1949. Oil. Painting in the manner of a child to portray a child, Picasso again demonstrates his incomprehensibility and charm.

75. *Playing.* 1950. Oil. Picasso's Private Collection. Claude, age three, plays with Paloma on an oriental-patterned floor. The daughter, named for the dove, was born in 1949.

76. *Chimneys of Vallauris.* 1951. Oil. Picasso's Private Collection. Spending most of his time in the making of ceramic sculptures, Picasso nevertheless took time out to paint this neo-realistic scene of the village near the Mediterranean. The chief occupations in this town were the making of ceramics and the manufacture of perfumes, both jobs requiring fire and creating smoke aplenty.

77. *View of the Mediterranean.* 1952. Oil. Private Collection. During periods of rest from his work at the kiln and in the studio where he modeled his ceramics, Picasso turned again to painting, producing many pleasant pictures of the town of Vallauris and its nearby seacoast, such as this.

78. *Massacre in Korea.* 1951. Oil. Painted as a protest against American support of the United Nations during the attempted Communist takeover of South Korea, this is another example of Picasso's politically-inspired works. Perhaps because he sensed that American "guilt" was not very clear-cut, if it existed at all, Picasso did not make clear whether the soldiers were American or Chinese and he did not make any great attempt to label the victims as Koreans. His Communist friends used the picture widely in anti-American propaganda. In 1956, however, anti-Communist students in Budapest displayed copies of the

picture with anti-Soviet slogans during the abortive Hungarian uprising in October of that year. Compare this work with *Guernica* (Plate 57).

79. *Portrait of Mme. H.P.* 1952. Oil. Influenced perhaps by his work in lithography during this period, Picasso attempted to combine his linear drawing technique with the distortion of surrealism.

80. *Seated Woman.* 1953. Oil. Freely combining the many aspects of his past work—cubism, surrealism and a touch of realism, Picasso paints vigorously, as usual, producing this rather wistful portrait.

81. *The Meal.* 1953. Oil. Picasso's Private Collection. Painted just before Francoise Gilot left him and returned to Paris with the children, leaving him alone in his Mediterranean studio. Devoted to his children, Picasso nevertheless found it difficult to stay with the same mistress or wife very long, his passionate nature never blending well with the extreme individualism of the women he invariably fancied.

82. *Sylvette.* 1954. Oil. Private Collection. One of twelve portraits painted of Sylvette Jellinek, the French wife of an Englishman living in Vallauris. She was a blonde, and her pony-tail seemed to exercise a great fascination for Picasso.

83. *Portrait of a Girl.* 1954. Picasso's Private Collection. Similar in style to his ceramic works are the lines in the background and the tones employed here. An entirely different way of portraying a girl (see Plate 82), demonstrating once again the versatility of the artist.

84. *Women of Algiers.* 1955. New York, Private Collection. Based on Delacroix's painting of the same name (1834), indicating Picasso's manner of improving on the old masters even while he attests to his admiration of their themes and styles. One of fifteen studies he did on the same theme, it reveals Picasso's ability to portray an erotic motive with his own brand of synthetic cubism. A masterpiece of composition, filled with emotions and hidden meanings, and all done in a masterfully elegant style.

85. *Maria Salimento.* 1957. Oil. Picasso's Private Collection. Based on the painting *Las Meninas* by Velasquez, showing the Infanta of

Spain entering the room where the artist was painting her father and mother (1656). This charming work, with Spanish overtones, shows Picasso's sense of the delicate in a superb manner.

86. *Children and Dog.* 1957. Picasso's Private Collection. Based again on the same composition by Velasquez ("Las Meninas" means "Ladies in Waiting"), and showing the Infanta, her young retinue and her dog. Here, however, Picasso forsakes Spanish colors and themes and instead brings alive the utter simplicity of children the world over.

87. *The Power of the Spirit and Life Over Evil.* 1958. Mural. Paris, UNESCO Headquarters. This large work, over 30 feet square, represents the artist's attempt to depict cultural enterprise in its broadest sense. Consisting of 40 panels, it now is placed on the wall of the hall leading to the Conference Room at the UNESCO complex.

88. *Balcony.* 1960. Oil. Picasso's Private Collection. Picasso painted only five pictures during the years 1960 and 1961 when he lived at Vauvenargues, a lonely estate which he bought in 1958, becoming, in fact, the Marquis de Vauvenargues, since he had purchased a chateau and the title went with it. During 1960, Picasso spent a great deal of time working on sculptures for a fountain.

89. *Lunch on the Grass.* 1961. Crayon. Although drawn on a small canvas, the lines are arranged so skilfully that the viewer has the feeling that the work is much larger than it really is. During this momentous year, Picasso celebrated his 80th birthday and married Jacqueline Roque.

PABLO RUIZ PICASSO

1881   Born at Malaga, Spain, on October 25, the son of José Ruiz Blasco, a painter, and Maria Picasso Lopez, of a prominent Malaga family. His full name at christening was Pablo Diego José Francisco de Paula Juan Nepomuceno Maria de los Remedios Cipriano de la Santisima Trinidad Ruiz y Picasso.

1889   Paints his first known work, *The Picador*.

1895   In October, the family settles in Barcelona, and although he is far too young, Picasso passes the entrance examination to the School of Fine Arts and is admitted to the highest class.

1897   By this time, his works have won prizes in Malaga. After a happy summer in Malaga, he leaves home alone for the first time, going to live in Madrid, where, in October, he enters the Royal Academy of San Fernando.

1898   Cut off from his uncle's patronage, he suffers greatly but paints many captivating portraits, including *Gypsy Girl on the Beach*.

1900   A little magazine reproduces a drawing, and in the fall, he moves to Paris with the painter Carlos Casagemas as his companion. In December, eager to improve the latter's failing health by exposure to Andalusian sunshine, the two return to Spain, where they settle in Malaga for ten days. In 1900, among other works, he paints *The Embrace*, in Paris.

1901   Leaving Casagemas in a Madrid tavern, Picasso founds a magazine *Young Art,* in conjunction with a friend, and publishes several issues until its demise. Around May, he returns to Paris via Barcelona and begins to paint furiously. An exhibit is held in Barcelona and another in Paris.
Among other works, he produces *Bibi la Purée, The Bullfight, Child Holding Pigeon, Figure of Jaime Sabartes, The Blue Room, Still Life on a Table* and *Woman's Face.* His Blue Period will last from 1901 to 1904.

1904   In April, Picasso leaves Catalonia for the last time and moves to Paris, where he is to make his home for many years. He meets Fernande Olivier, with whom he is to live for eight years. They nearly starve, as Picasso refuses to sell his works publicly and will not take on illustrating jobs.

1905   He begins to attract a few patrons, notably Gertrude and Leo Stein. The paintings of the next two years, 1905 and 1906, are usually labelled as those of "the Rose Period." Among them are: *Acrobat on a Ball, Girl will a Basket of Flowers* and *Seated Harlequin.*

1907   His radical departure from the past is marked by *Les Demoiselles d'Avignon,* criticized by all his friends. It is the first painting in which he is entirely himself, although influenced by Cézanne and perhaps by El Greco. In 1907, in addition to the *Women of Avignon,* he paints *Flowers on a Table* and *Head of a Girl.*

1912   His relationship with Fernande comes to an end in the spring, and he then takes as his companion Eva Gouel. They spend the summer at Sorgues-sur-l'Ouvèze, where he paints an early *Ma Jolie* on a wall, shipping the piece of wall back to Paris when he leaves.

1914   The war has little effect on Picasso, who continues his experiments with cubism. Among his works this year are *The Card Player* and another version of *Ma Jolie.*

1915   In the winter of 1915, Eva dies and Picasso is heartbroken. Among his few paintings of the year is *View with Still Life.*

1917   Jean Cocteau persuades Picasso to go to Italy to design costumes and scenery for Diaghilev's Russian Ballet. The work, *Parade,* is presented in Paris in May and the artists are nearly attacked by an outraged audience. Later, Picasso goes with the troupe on tour to Spain. Among Picasso's works of this year is *Italian Woman.*

1918   Picasso marries the ballerina Olga Koklova in July and the couple moves to the rue la Boètie. His best friend, Apollinaire, dies of influenza as the war ends.

1919   After another success with the Russian Ballet in London, where his sets for the *Three-Cornered Hat* are well-received, Picasso designs scenery and costumes for *Pulcinella.* The summer is spent in San Raphael. 1919 works include *The Balcony, School Girl,* and *Still Life on Bureau.*

1921   His son Paul (also known as Paulo) is born in February. The summer is spent at a villa near Fontainebleau, where he paints two versions of *Three Musicians.* The first important exhibition of Picasso's works is held in London.

1922   The summer is spent in Brittany and the neo-classical trend continues. Among his works: two versions of the theme, *Mother and Child* and *Still Life with Fish.*

1925   The *Women of Avignon* is reproduced for the first time and

Picasso's interest in surrealism becomes intense. In 1925, he paints *Paul as Pierrot, Three Dancers* and *Paul's Face*.

1926–27   Growing distortions occupy his canvas. The summer of 1927 is spent at Cannes. *Seated Woman* is painted in 1927.

1930–31   These two years see a flurry of sculpturing activity. Three exhibits in New York in 1931, one in London.

1932   In an outburst of energy, Picasso returns to painting. His works include *The Dream, Girl Before a Mirror* and *Sleeping Nude*.

1935   His mistress, Marie-Thérèse Walter, gives birth to a daughter, who is called Maia, and the artist dabbles with poetry. Jaime Sabartes returns to live with him for a time. One painting from 1935 is *The Muse*.

1936   His first exhibition in Spain since 1902 is held in Barcelona, Bilbao and Madrid.

1937   After the destruction of Guernica on April 29th, Picasso begins his masterpiece, intended as a mural for the Spanish Pavilion at the World's Fair in Paris. When it is finished he returns to Mougins with Dora Maar, his new mistress.
In addition to *Guernica,* 1937 sees Picasso produce *Face and Pitcher* and *Portrait of Marie-Thérèse*.

1939   After suffering from sciatica in the winter of 1938–39, Picasso returns to work. The summer is spent in Antibes, and his great work, *Night Fishing at Antibes* is finished the day before World War II breaks out. Aside from the above-mentioned work, Picasso in 1939 paints *Cat and Bird* and *Girl Holding Boat*.

1940–45   After a few months at Royan, Picasso returns to Paris in August, 1940, where he spends the rest of the war unmolested by the Nazis. In 1941 he writes a play, *Desire Caught by the Tail*. He sculpts, and refuses all offers of privileges tendered him by the Occupation Forces. Shortly after the Liberation of Paris, he becomes a Communist Party member.

During this period, he produces, among others, *Nude Dressing Her Hair, Skull of Bull on a Table, Portrait of Dora Maar, Tomato and Pitcher, Paris Landscape* and *Still Life*.

1948–50   Ceramics and politics occupy a great part of Picasso's time in this period. For the 1949 meeting in Paris of the Communist-sponsored World Peace Congress, he designs his famous white pigeon of peace. In 1947, a son, Claude, is born to Francoise, and in 1949, a daughter, Paloma. Picasso settles down in Vallauris in a pink villa, "La Galloise." He is deeply involved in family life. During this period, he paints *Kitchen, Claude* and *Playing*.

1951–54   The highlight of this period is his two-month marathon paint-. ing of *War and Peace* for the chapel at Vallauris. He visits Paris frequently. In November, 1953, his good friend Paul Eluard dies. In the summer of 1953, Francoise leaves him, taking the children with her. He enters a period of great despair.

Among his works of this period are *Massacre in Korea, Chimneys of Vallauris, View of the Mediterranean, Portrait of Mme. H. P., Seated Woman, The Meal, Silhouette* and *Portrait of a Girl*.

1955–66   Overwhelmed by his role as a famous man, Picasso finally has to take up permanent residence outside Paris, moving to La Californie, an Edwardian villa outside Cannes. His new mistress, Jacqueline Roque, helps him to make it liveable, but in 1958, he moves again, this time purchasing a huge property, the Chateau de Vauvenargues. He commutes between the two properties until later, when he abandons La Californie and takes a new villa, Le Mas Notre Dame de Vie, near Mougins. In March, 1961, he marries Jacqueline Roque.

Among the works he has painted since 1955 are *Women of Algiers, Maria Salimento, Children and Dog, The Power of the Spirit and Life Over Evil, Balcony* and *Lunch on the Grass.*

LIST OF COLOR PLATES

61.	Girl with a Cock. 1938.	76.	Chimneys of Vallauris. 1951.
62.	Cat with Bird. 1939.	77.	View of the Mediterranean. 1952.
63.	Girl Holding Boat. 1939.	78.	Massacre in Korea. 1951.
64.	Night Fishing at Antibes. 1939.	79.	Portrait of Madame H.P. 1952.
65.	Nude Dressing Her Hair. 1940.	80.	Seated Woman. 1953.
66.	Skull of Bull on a Table. 1942.	81.	The Meal. 1953.
67.	Portrait of Dora Maar. 1943.	82.	Sylvette. 1954.
68.	Tomato and Pitcher. 1944.	83.	Portrait of a Girl. 1954.
69.	Paris Landscape. 1945.	84.	Women of Algiers. 1955.
70.	Still Life. 1945.	85.	Maria Salimento. 1957.
71.	Joy of Life 1946.	86.	Children and Dog. 1957.
72.	Seated Woman. 1947.	87.	The Power of the Spirit and Life Over Evil. 1958.
73.	Kitchen. 1948.	88.	Balcony. 1960.
74.	Claude. 1949.	89.	Lunch on the Grass. 1961.
75.	Playing. 1950.		

THE PLATES

1 *Gypsy Girl on the Beach.* 1898. Oil. Paris, Private Collection. Painted when Picasso was 17 and a student at the Barcelona Art School.

2 *The Embrace.* 1900. Oil. 20⅝″ × 21⅝″. Moscow, Pushkin State Museum of Fine Arts. The subject—a prostitute and her client—was a common one in Picasso's early work.

3 *Bibi la Purée.* 1901. Oil on wood. 19½″ × 15⅜″. Paris, Private Collection. Somewhat influenced by Lautrec, he began to use more vivid colors and a broader touch.

4 *The Bullfight.* 1901. Oil. 18⅛″ × 21⅝″. Private Collection. This is the first statement of a theme that would later preoccupy Picasso.

5 *Child Holding a Dove.* 1901. Oil. 29″ × 21¼″. London, Private Collection. The sentimentality of this subject heralds an attitude typical of the Blue Period.

6 *Figure of Jaime Sabartés*. 1901. 31⅞″×25½″. Moscow, Museum of Western Art. The firmly drawn, fluid contours are characteristic of the Blue Period in its early months.

7   *The Blue Room.*   1901. Oil. 20″ × 24½″.   Washington, Phillips Gallery.   A picture of the room he occupied in the Boulevard de Clichy, Paris.

8 *Still Life on a Table*. 1901. Oil. 23⅛″ × 31¼″. Barcelona, Museum of Modern Art. The highly decorative objects of this composition indicate the influence of Gauguin.

9 *Woman's Face.* 1901. Oil. 20⅝″ × 13¼″. Otterlo, Rijksmuseum Kröller-Müller. Suggestions of Toulouse-Lautrec compete here with evidences of city sophistication.

10 *Mother and Child*. 1902—3. Pastel. 14⅜″ × 18⅛″. Private Collection. A familiar Blue-period subject, but stylistically reminiscent here of Degas and Impressionism generally.

11 *Mother and Child.* 1903. Pastel. 20¼″ × 15⅜″. Barcelona, Museum of Modern Art. A recurring theme of the Blue Period is the love of a mother for her desolate child.

12 *Celestina.* 1903. Oil. 31⅞″ × 23⅝″. Private Collection. A grotesque blind eye makes this masterpiece of realistic portraiture also an emotionally disturbing statement.

13 *Acrobat on a Ball.* 1904—05. Oil. 57⅜″×38⅛″. Moscow, Pushkin Museum of Fine Arts. Picasso moves gradually toward brighter and more active emotions and colors.

14 *Girl with a Basket of Flowers*. 1905. Oil. 59¾″ × 25½″. Gertrude Stein Collection. The latent classicism of the Rose period is clearly stated in the firm, clear drawing.

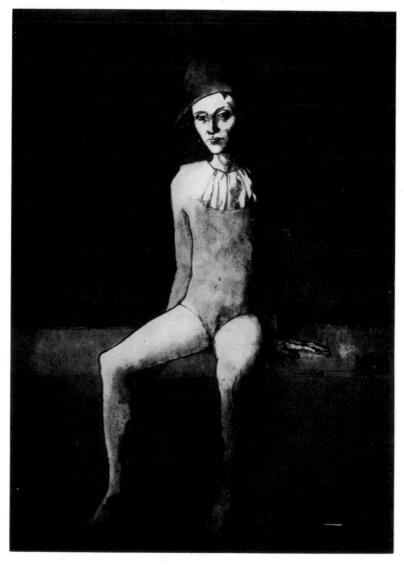

15 *Seated Harlequin.* 1905. Oil. Paris, Private Collection. Characteristic of the Rose Period is the disillusioned sadness and emaciation of the Harlequin type.

16 *Two Nudes*. 1906. Oil. 59⅜″×39¼″. Switzerland, Private Collection. A new sculptural power is seen here, inspired by both classical and Iberian statues.

17 *Peach-Colored Nude.* 1906. Oil. An interesting synthesis of Iberian plastic power and the earlier expressive sadness and withdrawal.

18 *Women of Avignon.* 1907. Oil. 96″ × 92″. New York, Museum of Modern Art. Definite hints of cubism, along with increasing simplification of detail, mark a new departure.

19 *Flowers on a Table*. 1907. Oil. 36½″ × 28½″. New York, Private collection. Picasso's primitivism of 1907 was so thoroughgoing that it could occur even in a still life.

20 *Head of a Girl*. 1907. Oil. 29⅜″ × 31⅞″. Paris, Private Collection. The stylized features and scarification of the nose clearly show the influence of African sculpture.

21 *Still Life with Gourd.* 1909. Oil. 28⅝″ × 23⅝″. Paris, Private Collection. Traces here of the influence of Cézanne, whom Picasso had admired since 1904.

22 *Pensive Harlequin.* 1909. Oil. 28⅝″ × 23¼″. Paris, Private Collection. A subject reminiscent of the Rose period, but treated in a more objective style.

23 *Girl with Mandolin.* 1901. Oil. 39¼″ × 28⅜″. New York, Private Collection. A characteristic
example of facet cubism, in which forms are reduced to clearly facetted volumes.

24 *Seated Woman in Armchair*. 1931. Oil. 57⅜″×38⅛″. Zurich, J. Eichmann Col. One of the earliest of Picasso's half-grotesque, half-comical representations of the female figure.

25 *Violin.* 1913. Oil. 25⅜″×18″. Berlin, Herman Rupp Collection. Typical of cubism around 1912 is the use of imitation wood graining and real sand (added to the paint).

26 *The Card Player*. 1913—14. Oil. 39¼″ × 31⅞″. New York, Museum of Modern Art. An example
of synthetic cubism, where flat, brightly colored planes predominate.

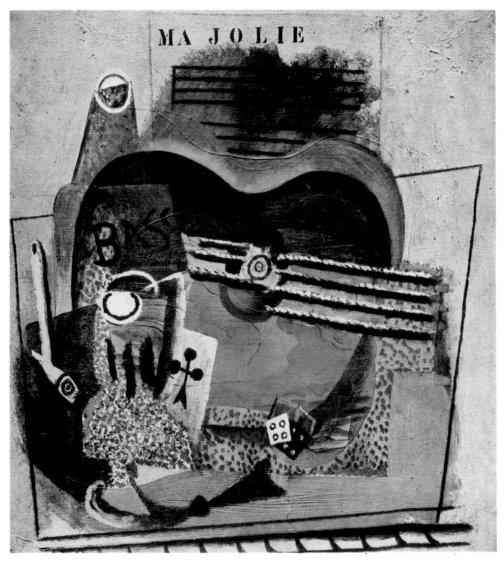

27   *Ma Jolie.*   1914. Oil. 17¾″ × 15¾″.   Paris, Private Collection.   The combination of objects found
in a cafe is typical of the cubist still life.

28 *Still Life Before Open Window*. 1915. Oil. 24⅜″ × 29⅜″. Paris, Private Collection. The pointillism of Seurat is here transformed into a decorative device.

29 *Italian Woman*.   1917. Oil. 58⅝″ × 39¾″.   Switzerland, Private Collection.   A romantic portrayal with Italian themes, reminiscent of Corot's Italian figures.

30 *Seated Harlequin.*   1918. Oil. 36⅛″ × 28⅝″.   New York, Museum of Modern Art.   A "theatrical" work both in content and in its flashy technique.

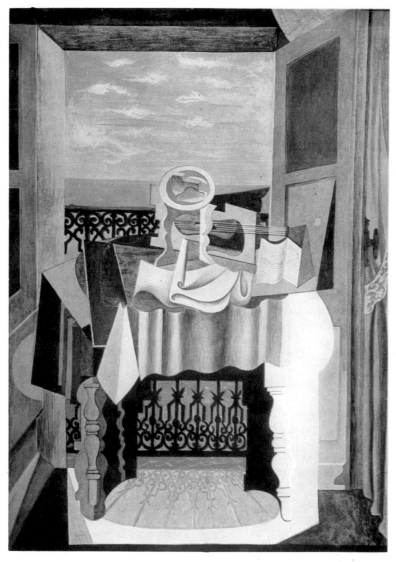

31 *The Balcony.* 1919. Oil. 9¾″ × 14¼″. New York, Museum of Modern Art. One of a large series in which indoor and outdoor spaces are juxtaposed.

32 *School Girl*. 1919. Oil. 36½″ × 29⅜″. London, Douglas Cooper Collection. An amusing characterization showing the expressive as well as formal power of cubism.

33 *Still Life on Bureau.* 1919. Oil. 31⅞″ × 39¼″. Picasso's Private Collection. One of the recurrent attempts by Picasso to rival an earlier style—here, the Baroque.

34 *Two Female Nudes*. 1920. Pastel. London, Douglas Cooper Collection. Typical of his interest in Greco-Roman art over a period of several years around 1920.

35 *Three Women at the Fountain.* 1920. Oil. 90½″ × 65⅛″. New York, Mus. of Mod. Art. An exaggerated, swollen classicism conceived perhaps in a spirit of rivalry with the antique.

36 *Still Life with Bird.* 1920. Pastel. 24⅜″ × 18½″. Paris, Private Collection. The dead creature introduces a disturbing note into this strongly patterned work.

37 *Three Musicians.* 1921. Oil. 81″×75″. Philadelphia, Museum of Art. Harlequin, Pierrot, and a Franciscan monk doubling as a jazz 'combo' of the 1920's.

38 *Mother and Child.* 1922. Oil. 39⅝″ × 31½″. Baltimore, Museum of Art. An example of his return
to an early sentimentality in treating a maternal theme.

39 *Mother and Child.* 1922. Oil. 38⅛″ × 27⅞″. New York, Private Collection. Contrast these heavy forms with his delicate approach in Plate 38.

40 *Still Life with Fish.* 1922—23. Oil. 41½″ × 32⅞″. Paris, National Museum of Modern Art.
Another still life before an open window, but with greater emphasis on the objects.

41 *Nude*. 1923. Pastel and crayon. 13¼″ × 9½″. Picasso's Private Collection. The classically fluid line is typical of one mode of Picasso's draughtmanship.

42 *Paul Drawing Pictures*.   1923.   Oil.   51″×38⅛″.   Picasso's   Private   Collection.   A   vividly naturalistic portrait, but clearly based on a cubist feeling for planes and lines.

43   *Paul as Pierrot*.   1925. Oil. 51″ × 38⅛″.   Picasso's Private Collection.   The garb of a clown, long one of Picasso's favorite costumes, is transferred here to his child.

44 *Still Life with Cake*. 1924. Oil. 39⅛″ × 51⅛″. New York, Museum of Modern Art. The sharply incised lines are probably inspired by Greek vase painting.

45 *View of a Port*.   1924. Oil. 15″×18⅛″.   Belgium, Private Collection.   A synthetic cubist work as intricately patterned as a Cézanne.

46　*Three Dancers*.　1925.　Oil.　84⅛″ × 54¾″.　Picasso's Private Collection.　Picasso in this period begins to paint in a more obviously surrealistic manner.

47 *Paul's Face.* 1925. Crayon and pastel. 9½″ × 6¼″. Picasso's Private Collection. A deliberately stylized line and soft open areas of color are juxtaposed.

48 *Seated Woman*. 1927. Oil 51″×38⅛″. Farmington, Private Collection. A haunting, even frightening image, close to Surrealism in its mood.

49 *Paul as Pierrot.* 1929. Oil. 51″ × 38⅛″. Picasso's Private Collection. The influence of Velasquez's portraits of royal children can be seen here.

50 *On the Beach*. 1928. Oil. 7⅜″×11¾″. New York, Museum of Modern Art. His sense of humor produces a bizarre, yet entirely intelligible image.

51 *The Dream.* 1932. Oil. 51″×38⅛″. New York, Private Collection. The curvilinear cubism of the early 1930's is evident in the swollen contours.

52 *Girl Before a Mirror*. 1932. Oil. 64″ × 54¾″. New York, Museum of Modern Art. The mirror functions metaphorically to reveal the hidden aspect of the personality.

53 *Sleeping Nude.* 1932. Oil. Similar in many ways to *Dream*, this contains hints of the kinds of dreams portrayed by El Greco and Goya.

54 *The Muse.* 1935. Oil. 51″×64″. Paris, National Museum of Modern Art. One of a large number of works in the 1930's in which the subject itself is the creation of art.

55 *Face and Pitcher*. 1937. Oil. An evocative juxtaposition of object and face, the latter half-transformed into an object itself.

56 *Portrait of Marie-Thérèse.* 1937. Oil. 39½″ × 31⅞″. Private Collection. Despite the distorted features, Picasso's appreciation of the model's physical beauty comes through.

57 *Guernica*. 1937. Mural. 138¼″ × 307⅝″.   New York, Mus. Modern Art.   Inspired by one event, the bombing of a Spanish town, the mural makes a powerful statement about modern war in general.

58 *Portrait of Maia*. 1938. Oil. 28⅝″ × 23⅝″. Picasso's Private Collection. A tender and amusing portrait of his daughter.

59   *The Cock*.   1938.   Pastel.   26¼″ × 18½″.   New York, Private Collection.   Another alter-ego of the artist, the cock is appropriately painted in intensely bright colors.

60 *Maia's Face*. 1938. Pastel. 9½″ × 7⅜″. Picasso's Private Collection. The tenderness with which he paints here is similar to that in *Paul's Face* (Plate 47).

61 *Girl with a Cock.* 1938. Oil. 57¼″ × 47¼″. New York, Private Collection. Picasso's disillusionment following the Spanish Civil War is expressed here in an unforgettable image.

62 *Cat and Bird.* 1939. Oil. 31⅞″ × 39¼″. Picasso's Private Collection. Foreshadowing the holocaust of World War II, the predatory cat reminds us of *Guernica.*

63 *Girl Holding a Boat*. 1939. Oil. 36¼″ × 28⅝″. Picasso's Private Collection. Picasso cleverly adapts a child's mode of drawing that is appropriate to the content.

64 *Night Fishing at Antibes.* 1939. Oil. 83⅞″ × 136″. New York, Museum of Modern Art. Painted on the eve of the war, this dramatic work combines humor and an eerie nocturnal atmosphere.

65 *Nude Dressing Her Hair*. 1940. Oil. 51″ × 38⅛″. Picasso's Private Collection. One of the most brutally distorted images of women in Picasso's works.

66 *Skull of Bull on a Table*.   1942. Oil. 50⅞″×38″.   Paris, Private Collection.   An appropriately grim war-time still life with macabre overtones.

67 *Portrait of Dora Maar.* 1943. Oil. 31½″ × 23¼″. Paris, Private Collection. A gentle deformation
of the natural represents an escape into the peaceful world of a woman.

68 *Tomato and Pitcher.* 1944. Oil. 28⅝″ × 36¼″. Picasso's Private Collection. The tomato plant, an allusion to war-time food shortages, is incorporated into a powerful cubist design.

69 *Paris Landscape.* 1945. Oil. 28⅝″ × 36¼″. Picasso's Private Collection. A cubist view of Notre
Dame appropriately marks the liberation of Paris.

70 *Still Life*. 1945. Oil. 8¾″ × 10⅝″. The more relaxed manner of Picasso's post-war work is heralded in this swiftly painted canvas.

71 *Joy of Life.* 1946. Mural. 47⅛″ × 98¼″. Antibes, Grimaldi Museum. The end of the war and Picasso's own sense of relief are obvious in this pseudo-classical romp.

72 *Seated Woman*. 1947. Oil. 51″ × 38⅛″. Picasso's Private Collection. A work reminiscent of the 1930's in its surrealistic view of the figure.

73 *Kitchen.* 1948. Oil. 68⅞″ × 98¼″. Picasso's Private Collection. A clear example of Picasso's power to transform entirely an insignificant motif.

74 *Claude.* 1949. Oil. 51″×38⅛″. Picasso's son by Francoise Gilot is now two years old; the artist himself seems a child as he lovingly draws this portrait.

75 *Playing.* 1950. Oil. 46¼″ × 57″. Picasso's Private Collection. Claude, age three, plays amid a complex jumble of forms showing a charming blend of patterns.

76 *Chimneys of Vallauris.* 1951. Oil. 23½″ × 28⅝″. Picasso's Private Coll. His use of cubism still apparent, Picasso nevertheless depicts this scene in terms nearly realistic.

77   *View of the Mediterranean.*   1952. Oil. 31⅞″ × 49⅛″.   Private Coll.   With these lush and brilliant colors, the artist expresses his joy in the Mediterranean color and light.

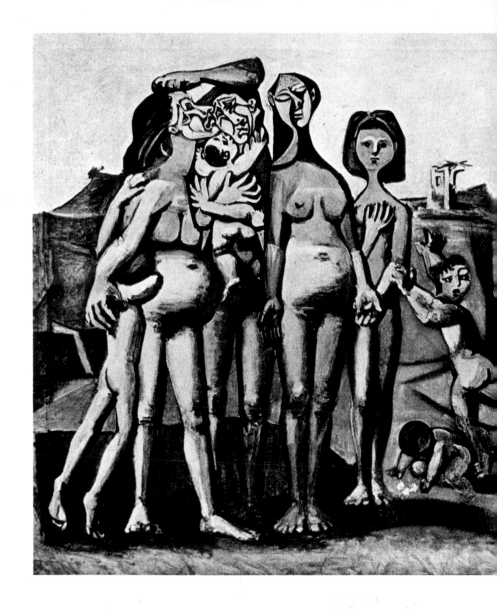

78 *Massacre in Korea.* 1951. Oil. 42⅞″ × 78⅞″. Reminiscent of Goya's *Executions of May 3rd*, but classical in form, this slaughter of the innocents is frankly political.

79 *Portrait of Madame H.P.* 1952. Oil. 57⅜″ × 37¾″. · Painted in the colors of Antibes, this is a remarkably penetrating portrayal of a woman of great character.

80 *Seated Woman*. 1953. Oil. 51″ × 37¾″. Demonstrating his versatility in the use of colors, Picasso paints a woman at once somber, delicate and imposing.

81 *The Meal*. 1953. Oil. 38⅛″ × 51″. Picasso's Private Collection. An intimate portrait of Picasso's own family at the table.

82 *Sylvette*. 1954. Oil. 45½″ × 35″. Private Collection. One of a series of works inspired by the classically pure features of a girl Picasso met in Vallauris.

83 *Portrait of a Girl*. 1954. Oil. 39¼″ × 31⅞″. Picasso's Private Collection. The same model as in the previous plate, but in a more introspective mood.

84 *Women of Algiers.* 1955. 44¾″×57⅜″. New York, Private Collection. Based on Delacroix's painting of 1834, it is one of a long series of remarkably inventive variations.

85 *Maria Salimento*. 1957. Oil. 45¼″×35″. Picasso's Private Collection. Based on a detail of the famous painting *Las Meninas* by Velasquez, showing the Infanta.

86 *Children and Dog*. 1957. Oil. 51″ × 37¾″. Picasso's Private Collection. Based on the same composition by Velasquez, treated now in a deliberately childish manner.

87 *The Power of the Spirit and Life Over Evil.* 1958. Mural. Paris, UNESCO Headquarters. A vast, yet sparsely composed mural, not entirely successful.

88 *Balcony*. 1960. Oil. 19⅝″ × 23¾″. Picasso's Private Collection. One of the nocturnal landscapes with doves seen from the artist's house at Cannes.

89 *Lunch on the Grass.* 1961. Crayon. 10⅝″ × 16⅛″. A study for one of the variations on Manet's revolutionary *Luncheon on the Grass* of 1863.